BLOOMSBURY CHILDREN'S BOOKS
Bloomsbury Publishing Inc., part of Bloomsbury Publishing Plc
1385 Broadway, New York, NY 10018

BLOOMSBURY, BLOOMSBURY CHILDREN'S BOOKS, and the Diana logo are trademarks of Bloomsbury Publishing Plc

First published in Great Britain in November 2018 by Bloomsbury Publishing Plc
Published in the United States of America in November 2018
by Bloomsbury Children's Books

Text by Teresa Heapy
Illustrations by Artful Doodlers
Text and illustrations copyright © 2018 by Bloomsbury Publishing Plc

Bloomsbury books may be purchased for business or promotional use. For information on bulk purchases please contact
Macmillan Corporate and Premium Sales Department at specialmarkets@macmillan.com

Library of Congress Cataloging-in-Publication Data
available upon request
ISBN 978-1-5476-0025-0 (hardcover) • ISBN 978-1-5476-0026-7 (e-book) • ISBN 978-1-5476-0027-4 (e-PDF)

Typeset in Garden Pro and Emily's Candy • Book design by Maia Fjord
Printed in China by Leo Paper Products, Heshan, Guangdong
2 4 6 8 10 9 7 5 3 1

All papers used by Bloomsbury Publishing Plc are natural, recyclable products made from wood grown in well-managed forests.
The manufacturing processes conform to the environmental regulations of the country of origin.

To find out more about our authors and books visit www.bloomsbury.com and sign up for our newsletters.

Princess Snowbelle
and the Snow Games

Libby Frost

BLOOMSBURY
CHILDREN'S BOOKS
NEW YORK LONDON OXFORD NEW DELHI SYDNEY

On a chilly but clear day in the kingdom of Frostovia, Princess Snowbelle stood by the frozen Opaline Lake with her brothers, Nicholas and Noel.

"Do you see them yet?" Noel asked eagerly.

Their friends from Snowland—Sparkleshine, Jonathan, and James—were coming to visit to participate in the annual Snow Games.

"I'm sure they'll arrive soon!" said Snowbelle.
"I hope we'll finally win the Ice Trophy this year."

Noel puffed out his chest. "I'll win the sled
race. I've added extra-fast runners to my sled.
NO ONE can beat me."

Nicholas started stretching. "And I'll win the
footrace. I trained for weeks."

Snowbelle played with her silver charm bracelet, hoping it would lend her some magic for her event—the horse race.

Just then, their parents returned from their daily twirl around the icy lake.

"Now, children," said their mother, "remember, it's not about winning. It's about trying your best!"

The children only grinned. After years of losing, they wanted to WIN!

Finally, the royal family of Snowland arrived!
Snowbelle embraced her best friend, Sparkleshine.
"It's so good to see you!" she said.

Snowbelle's father clapped his hands.
"And now—let the Snow Games begin!"

The Games began with the sled race, which started at the top of the tallest sledding hill.

Noel took off fast . . .

Too fast! His super-speedy runners sent his sled spinning out of control, and he tumbled over in a heap of snow.

James won the race!

As Noel sulked, James comforted him. "You did well—it's just bad luck."

"Don't worry," added Nicholas. "We can still win the Games!"

The children lined up for the footrace.
"Go twice around the lake," called Snowbelle's
mother. "Ready . . . set . . . GO!"

Nicholas sped off in a blur, leaving
only windswept snowflakes in his wake.
He finished the two laps before the
others even finished one!

Snowbelle and Noel cheered.

"Good job, Nicholas!" cried Snowbelle.
"Now it's a tie!"

"Yes, well done," said Jonathan.

The third event was Snowbelle's specialty—a horse race through the forest.

She mounted her snow-white horse, Icetail. Next to her, Sparkleshine rode Crystalmane, a piebald with a glittery midnight mane.

Snowbelle smoothed Icetail's mane. "We can do this! The whole family is counting on us."

"Are you ready?" called Snowbelle's father. "On your mark . . . get set . . . GO!"

Both horses set off at a gallop, sending up clouds of snow with each pound of their hooves. Sparkleshine raced ahead. Snowbelle clung on tightly as Icetail dodged through the trees.

But suddenly . . .

Disaster!

The edge of Snowbelle's velvet cape caught on a low-hanging branch, and Icetail jolted to a stop. They couldn't move!

They watched as Sparkleshine and
Crystalmane raced ahead.

Snowbelle's heart sank. "Oh no.
We'll never win now, Icetail. Noel and
Nicholas will be so disappointed."

But then something glittered in the distance, and a girl on a horse appeared—Sparkleshine and Crystalmane, racing back to rescue them!

"Hold on," said Sparkleshine. She carefully unhooked the cape, setting Snowbelle free.

"I can't believe you came back!" cried Snowbelle. "You would have won."

Sparkleshine smiled. "I couldn't leave my best friend behind! Let's finish together!"

The two girls crossed the finish line side by side. Their families rushed forward, relieved to see them safe.

"We were worried about you two!" said Noel. "Sparkleshine saved me," said Snowbelle. "She's the best friend ever."

SNOW GAMES

Sledding 🛡 Snowland

Running 👑 Frostovia

Sn... S...

The judges declared the horse race
a draw, which meant the winner of
the final round—the Snow Sculpture
contest—would also win the Snow Games.
Even though she wanted that trophy
badly, Snowbelle looked at Sparkleshine
and remembered her friend's kindness.

"Winning doesn't matter!" Snowbelle said. "Let's all
work together and make the best snow sculpture ever!"
"That's a great idea!" said Nicholas.

So the children worked as a team to build the grandest, most magical snow palace they could imagine.

Their sculpture had dozens of tiny windows and a grand door with a drawbridge, and tall towers with delicate, icy turrets decorated the top.

The children stood back to admire their work.
"It's *beautiful*," breathed Snowbelle.

The kings and queens of Frostovia and Snowland turned to their children.

"This is the grandest snow sculpture we've seen in any Snow Games!" said the queen of Snowland.

"We are very proud that you all worked together as a team," said the king of Snowland. "So, we've decided that the Ice Trophy is yours to share!"

They all cheered as Snowbelle's mother lifted the shimmering cup made of crystalline ice. Tiny, shining snowflakes decorated the cup's edges.

Noel rushed over to his mother. "Can I hold it?"

In his excitement, Noel reached out and knocked the trophy from her hands. It hit the cold, snowy ground and shattered into pieces. Everyone gasped.

"Oh no!" cried Noel. "I'm so sorry."

Snowbelle noticed her silver charm bracelet glowing slightly around her wrist, and she had an idea.

"Don't worry!" she said. "I can fix it!"

She shook the delicate bracelet once . . . twice . . . and with a little chime of bells . . .
The Ice Trophy pieces came back together again!

Everyone cheered and hugged one another.
"And now, I think we all deserve a treat," announced Snowbelle's father.

The spectators came to join the
celebrations, and the palace cook appeared
with trays of cookies and steaming hot cocoa.

"Don't forget the trophy," Snowbelle's mother said, smiling.

"Let's both hold it, Sparkleshine," said Snowbelle, and they lifted the cup high together.

"This belongs to ALL of us!"